Desert Critter Friends

Clubhouse Surprises

Mona Gansberg Hodgson
Illustrated by Chris Sharp

CPH®
SAINT LOUIS

Dedicated to my daughters, Amy and Sara,
whose love inspires me.

Desert Critter Friends Series

Friendly Differences

Thorny Treasures

Sour Snacks

Smelly Tales

Clubhouse Surprises

Desert Detectives

Scripture quotations taken from the HOLY BIBLE, NEW INTERNATIONAL VERSION®. NIV®. Copyright © 1973, 1978, 1984 by International Bible Society. Used by permission of Zondervan Publishing House. All rights reserved.

Copyright © 1999 Mona Gansberg Hodgson

Published by Concordia Publishing House
3558 S. Jefferson Avenue, St. Louis, MO 63118-3968
Manufactured in the United States of America

Library of Congress Cataloging-in-Publication Data

Hodgson, Mona Gansberg, 1954–
    Clubhouse surprises / Mona Gansberg Hodgson ; illustrated by Chris Sharp.
        p.   cm. — (Desert critter friends series ; bk 5)
    Summary: Fergus the owl helps the other members of the Desert Critter Friends Club see how they can all work together to make a clubhouse everyone can enjoy. Additional text explains how Jesus helps us cooperate and love one another.
    ISBN 0-570-05082-0
    [1. Owls—Fiction. 2. Desert animals—Fiction. 3. Clubs—Fiction. 4. Christian life—Fiction.] I. Sharp, Chris, 1954– ill. II. Title. III. Series: Hodgson, Mona Gansberg, 1954– Desert critter friends ; bk. 5.
PZ7.H6649Cl   1999
[E]—dc21
                                                    98-27990
                                                    AC

1 2 3 4 5 6 7 8 9 10   08 07 06 05 04 03 02 01 00 99

Fergus, the great horned owl,
rested in a cottonwood tree. Turning
his fuzzy head, he watched as his
friends gathered in the shade below
him. It was time for the Desert
Critter Friends to have a meeting.

Fergus watched Bert, the road-runner, and Taylor, the tortoise, get ready for the meeting. Lenny, the pack rat, and Jill, the ground squirrel, scurried over to talk to Myra, the quail, and Rosie, the skunk. Fergus listened.

"The place Bert and Rosie found
for us to put our clubhouse is
perfect," Lenny said. "We can use
logs to make it nice and cozy."

"*Achoo!*" Rosie sneezed.

Myra looked at Rosie. "A log won't work," she said. "Some of us have lots of fur. We wouldn't all fit. I think a big bush would make a perfect clubhouse. A dirt floor covered with twigs would be comfy."

Fergus watched Toby and Wanda, the cottontail rabbits, hop up.

"Our clubhouse can't be in a bush," Wanda warned. "A coyote would find us."

"We could dig a nice, big hole for the clubhouse," her brother Toby said. "That would be safer for us."

"A hole won't do," Bert said, zooming over. "I need to stay above ground. I like to be *on* the road, not under it."

"Bert's a roadrunner, not a hole-crawler," Jamal, the jackrabbit, reported.

"*Ha! Ha! Ha!*" Bert laughed.

"*He! He! Ha!*" Wanda laughed.

"*Ho! Ho! Ha!*" Lenny laughed.
Then everybody laughed.

"What about a treehouse?"
Fergus called down from his
branch. "It would be safe and we
could spy on everything!"

All the friends looked up at Fergus.

"A tree house is *too* far above the ground," Bert said.

Jamal looked down at his big back feet. "Some of us weren't made to fly." Then he looked at the tortoise. "And Taylor would have trouble climbing a tree."

"*Achoo!*" Rosie, the skunk, sneezed. "I'm sure we can build something we will all like," she said. "We just have to work together."

Flap. Flap. Flap. Fergus flew to a higher branch. He pouted and stuck out the lower part of his beak. His friends just didn't see things the way he did.

Smack! Taylor hit the tree stump with a stick. Fergus watched. *Smack! Smack!* The critters still chattered.

Zoom! Screech! Bert zipped over to the stump and whistled. The friends grew quiet. Bert nodded his head at the tortoise.

Taylor pushed his glasses up on his nose. "As meeting moderator—"

"What is a *motor-later*?" asked Jill, the ground squirrel.

"A leader," Bert said. "And it's not *motor*. *Mod* rhymes with *God*. *MODerator* means leader."

Taylor started again. "As meeting moderator, I call to order this meeting of the Desert Critter Friends Club."

Fergus didn't hear what Taylor said next. He was still pouting. Lenny lived in a log. Toby, Wanda, and Rosie lived underground. Myra and Bert lived in bushes. Taylor lived in a shallow hole in the ground. None of his desert critter friends lived in a tree.

What was so bad about living high in a tree? Fergus thought. There was so much to see. He looked down at Taylor.

The tortoise pushed his glasses up on his nose. He read his book, *Robert's Rules of Order*. Then Taylor said, "Now I call upon Bert, the chairman of the clubhouse committee, to give us his report."

Zoom! Bert zoomed to the front of the group. "As you know, we had a race to decide which team would build the Critter Clubhouse. Wanda and Toby tied the race. Toby said we could all work together on the clubhouse. Everyone agreed!"

All the friends cheered. Except Fergus.

18

"I'll be in charge of the building project," Bert said. "When we decide what kind of clubhouse we want, Taylor will draw the plans. Then we'll need workers."

"I can dig," Wanda shouted.

"I can carry water," Rosie said.

"I can find sticks," Toby called out.

Fergus stared at his claws. His feet couldn't dig, or carry, or build. What would he do?

Pound. Pound. Pound. Taylor hit the stump with his stick. He waved his book at the critter crowd. "We're not following the rules. Someone needs to make a motion that we give out the jobs ..."

"Rules, *shmools*," Fergus grumbled. Why was he at this meeting, anyway? Why was he out in the sunshine at all? It was way past his bedtime. But he was too upset to sleep. Fergus flapped his wings and flew away.

Fergus landed in a tree by the place Bert and Rosie had found for them to build the clubhouse. His fuzzy head twisted back and forth.

A good place for a clubhouse, Fergus thought. He could spy a lot from here. "Even *if* I'm the only one who cares about that," he mumbled.

Fergus saw a log for Lenny.
Bushes for Bert and Myra. And he
liked this tree. But they needed
a place where they could all
come together—work together.
Was that even possible?

Fergus blinked three times.
Blink. Blink. Blink. He saw something
he hadn't noticed before.

It was a hole in the hillside.
And a sign. Fergus flew to the sign.
It said: *Little Daisy Mine.*

Fergus peeked inside the hole.
"Wow!" he said. "What a great
cave!" It would be cozy and comfy.
And his tree was right outside. This
cave could make a great clubhouse!

Fergus heard someone coming. He flew back up into the cottonwood tree. Bert zoomed into view. The roadrunner pulled his measuring tape out of his backpack.

"Bert!" Fergus shouted.

Bert jumped. "Fergus? We wondered where you went."

"*Here* is where I went," Fergus said. "All that talk about drawing and digging and carrying. I can't do any of it. So I left."

"Sorry, Fergus. I'm sure there's something you can do. I have to measure," Bert said.

Fergus flew to Bert. "I have a surprise for you. Something you'll want to explore."

"Something to explore?" Bert looked around. His tape measure snapped shut. "Where is it?" he asked.

"In that hillside." Fergus pointed toward the sign. "It's a hole in the hill."

"It is?" Bert tipped his head. "I don't see anything!"

"You have to explore to find it." Fergus flew to the opening. "It's right here behind these bushes."

Bert zoomed to the hole in the hillside. "Wow!" he shouted as he

ran inside the cave. Fergus
followed him.

"This is a great surprise,
Fergus! We can all work
together to make our clubhouse!"

"That's what I
thought," Fergus
said.

31

Bert zoomed around, measuring. "We can pull a log in here for Lenny."

"Toby and Wanda can dig a hole in that wall," Fergus added, pointing with his wing.

"There's even room for me to zoom," Bert said. "But ..." He stopped. "There's no tree."

Fergus landed in front of Bert. Bert did care what he liked. He was a good friend.

"That's okay," Fergus said. "The cottonwood tree is right outside. And I can perch on Lenny's log."

"Well, friend," Bert said, "you found just the right spot for our clubhouse. Maybe you can't dig or carry, but you can spy better than any of us."

Fergus winked. He was a great spy.

Bert zoomed outside. Fergus flew behind him. "I'll go tell our friends," Bert said.

Fergus yawned. "I'd better go home and take a nap. I'm not used to staying awake during the day."

"Okay. See you later!" *Zoom!*

Flap. Flap. Flap. Fergus flew home.

Fergus took a long nap. When he woke up, he was full of questions.

Had his friends gone to the cave? Did they think it would make a good clubhouse? Would they all find a way to work together? Fergus scratched his fuzzy head.

Spreading his wings, Fergus flew into the moonlight. He landed in the cottonwood tree outside the cave.

Fergus looked at the cave. It had a new sign: *Desert Critter Friends' Clubhouse*.

"I guess they liked it," Fergus mumbled as he flew inside.

"SURPRISE! SURPRISE!" the critters all shouted.

Fergus looked around at his friends. They had moved in! There was a log for Lenny. Toby and Wanda had started digging a hole. Myra had spread out twigs. Just then Fergus froze.

Fergus blinked. *Blink! Blink! Blink!* A tree! His friends had set up a tree for him in the middle of the cave! He had been wrong. They *did* care about him. They *could* work together, even though they didn't always see things in the same way. A happy tear slid down his beak. Fergus flew to a branch on his clubhouse tree.

Lenny scurried over to the tree. "It's cozy and homey," he said. "And now you have a place where you can spy."

"Three cheers for Fergus," Rosie shouted. "He found the perfect place for our clubhouse."

"HIP HIP HOORAY! HIP HIP HOORAY! HIP HIP HOORAY!"

Fergus twisted his head to look at all his friends. Another happy tear slid down his beak.

Jesus is your very best friend. He died on a cross so that you can live with Him forever. He will help you love your friends. He will help you cooperate.

Live in harmony with one another. Romans 12:16

Hi kids!

Bert knows how to make twenty-five words from ROADRUNNER. How many words can you make?

ROADRUNNER

and _____

_____

_____

_____

_____

_____

_____

_____

_____

_____

_____

_____

_____

_____

_____

_____

_____

_____

_____

_____

_____

_____

For Parents and Teachers:

We've all experienced frustration when our family members, friends, or coworkers haven't understood our perspective. We've had our feelings hurt when it seemed they didn't care what we thought. At times, we've pouted and stomped off (at least emotionally) when we didn't get our way. We've all felt left out, maybe even inadequate, when we felt our talents didn't match up with those of our friends.

Fergus couldn't dig or carry, but he could explore from a different perspective than that of his friends. In the end, the differences he thought had alienated him gave him the opportunity to make a valuable contribution to the clubhouse project.

God has richly blessed us in making us uniquely individual in our perspective and in our abilities. Paul teaches in Romans 12, and 1 Corinthians 12, that we are all parts of one body. Jesus has united us in that body—the Church—by sacrificing Himself for us. He is the head of the body, the living example who helps us share His love with one another. An even greater purpose can be fulfilled when we work together as the church of Christ, with all the parts making their special contribution.

Help your children understand that God doesn't want us to focus on what we can't do. Instead, He will help us celebrate and develop our varying interests and abilities as we cooperate with others and work together. Think of some ways your children can use their abilities to cooperate in sharing Jesus' love.

Here are some questions and activities you can use as discussion starters to help your children understand these concepts.

Discussion Starters

1. Why couldn't the Desert Critter Friends decide what kind of clubhouse to build?

2. Why did Fergus pout? Why did he feel left out?

3. Have you ever felt left out? What did you do?

4. Fergus couldn't dig or carry. What was he able to do that his friends couldn't do? How did that make him a part of the clubhouse project?

5. What special talents do your friends (or brothers and sisters) have? What special talents has God given you?

6. How did Fergus' friends show him they cared about him? How can you use your talents to show your friends that you care about them?

Pray together. Thank God for sending His Son to make you a part of His family. Ask God to forgive you for those times when you have pouted because you didn't get to do things your way. Ask God to help you live out His love as you cooperate with your family and friends.

Jesus will help you cooperate with your friends. What would you like to do together? Tell me by writing on these lines.

_____

_____

_____

_____